potato

pepper

chard

radish

pumpkin

sunflower

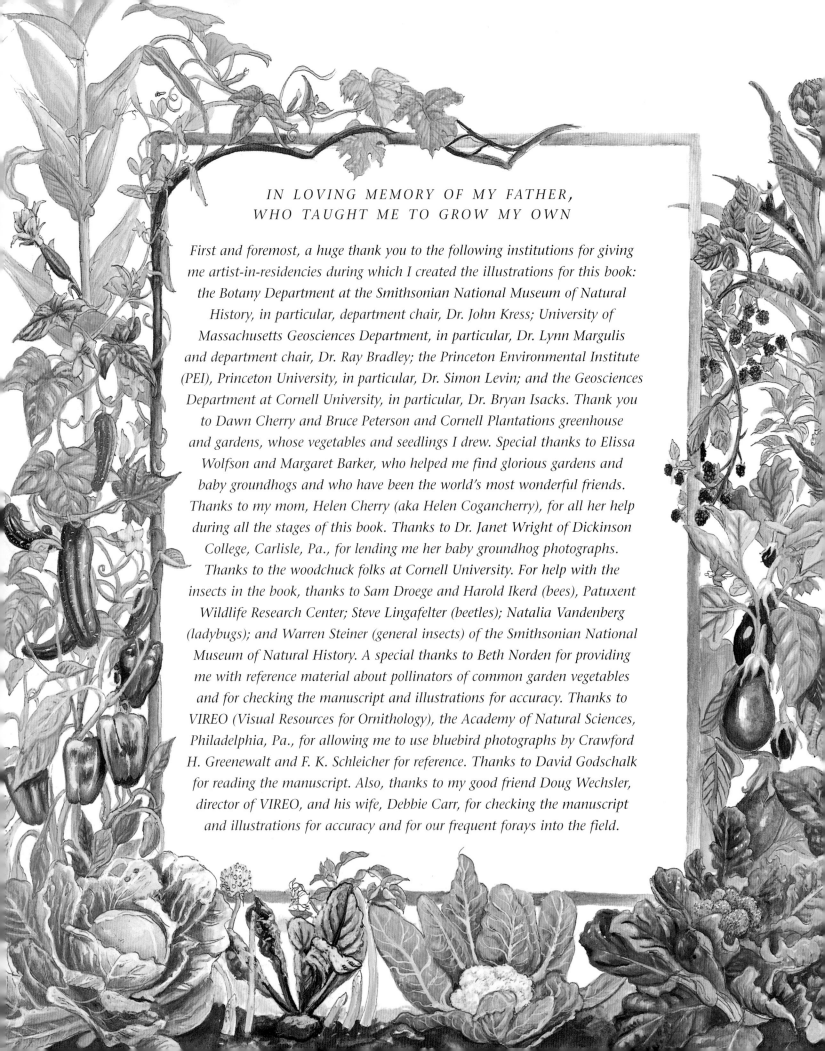

IN LOVING MEMORY OF MY FATHER,
WHO TAUGHT ME TO GROW MY OWN

First and foremost, a huge thank you to the following institutions for giving me artist-in-residencies during which I created the illustrations for this book: the Botany Department at the Smithsonian National Museum of Natural History, in particular, department chair, Dr. John Kress; University of Massachusetts Geosciences Department, in particular, Dr. Lynn Margulis and department chair, Dr. Ray Bradley; the Princeton Environmental Institute (PEI), Princeton University, in particular, Dr. Simon Levin; and the Geosciences Department at Cornell University, in particular, Dr. Bryan Isacks. Thank you to Dawn Cherry and Bruce Peterson and Cornell Plantations greenhouse and gardens, whose vegetables and seedlings I drew. Special thanks to Elissa Wolfson and Margaret Barker, who helped me find glorious gardens and baby groundhogs and who have been the world's most wonderful friends. Thanks to my mom, Helen Cherry (aka Helen Cogancherry), for all her help during all the stages of this book. Thanks to Dr. Janet Wright of Dickinson College, Carlisle, Pa., for lending me her baby groundhog photographs. Thanks to the woodchuck folks at Cornell University. For help with the insects in the book, thanks to Sam Droege and Harold Ikerd (bees), Patuxent Wildlife Research Center; Steve Lingafelter (beetles); Natalia Vandenberg (ladybugs); and Warren Steiner (general insects) of the Smithsonian National Museum of Natural History. A special thanks to Beth Norden for providing me with reference material about pollinators of common garden vegetables and for checking the manuscript and illustrations for accuracy. Thanks to VIREO (Visual Resources for Ornithology), the Academy of Natural Sciences, Philadelphia, Pa., for allowing me to use bluebird photographs by Crawford H. Greenewalt and F. K. Schleicher for reference. Thanks to David Godschalk for reading the manuscript. Also, thanks to my good friend Doug Wechsler, director of VIREO, and his wife, Debbie Carr, for checking the manuscript and illustrations for accuracy and for our frequent forays into the field.

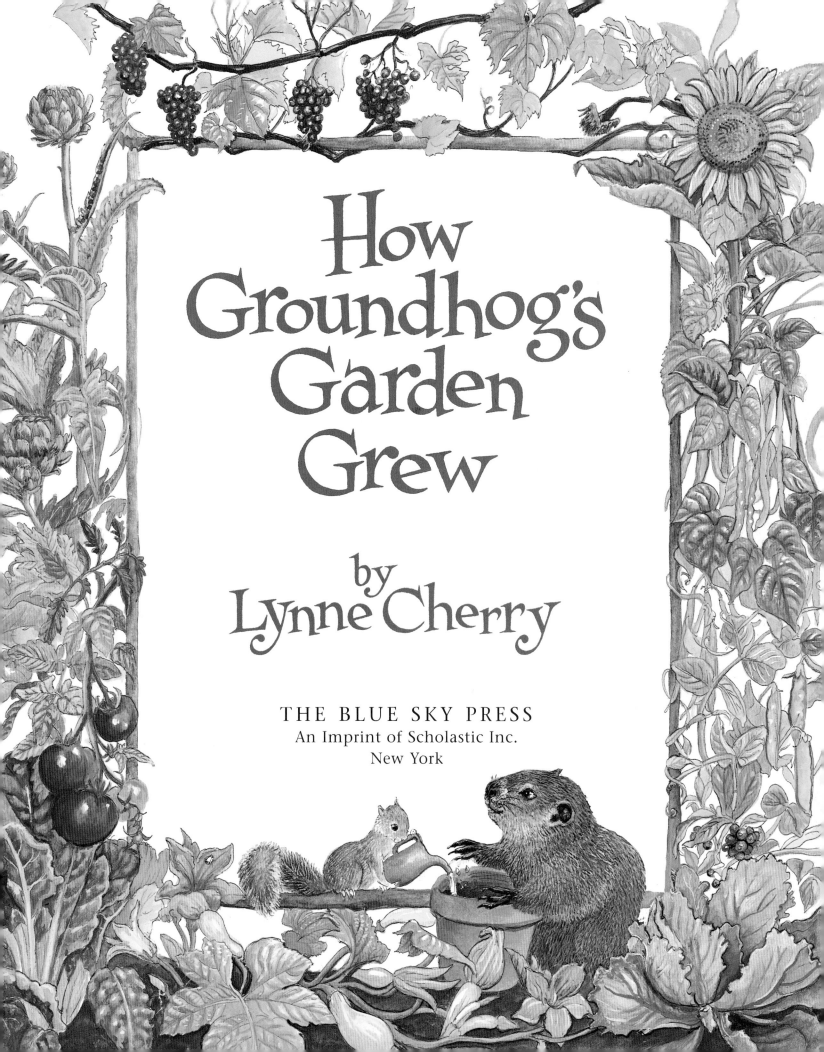

How Groundhog's Garden Grew

by Lynne Cherry

THE BLUE SKY PRESS
An Imprint of Scholastic Inc.
New York

Little Groundhog was hungry. "Beautiful! Scrumptious! Irresistible!" he exclaimed as he crept into a neighbor's lovely vegetable garden. He was nibbling on some fresh green lettuce when Squirrel rushed down from her tree.

"Little Groundhog!" Squirrel scolded. "This food does not belong to you. If you take food that belongs to others, you will not have a friend in the world! Why don't you plant your OWN garden?"

"I'm sorry," Little Groundhog told her, embarrassed, "but I don't know how."

"Well, then," replied Squirrel, "I will show you."

Lima beans

onion sets

Lima beans

cantaloupe

radish

sweet
pepper
seeds

squash seeds

Lima beans

sunflower seeds

"First, you will need seeds," said Squirrel.
Little Groundhog helped Squirrel
and her friends pick beans and peas
from pods, and seeds from a
sunflower's drooping head.

peas

asparagus
seeds

They collected seeds from inside
peppers, cantaloupes, cucumbers,
and tomatoes.

Squirrel chewed a hole into a
pumpkin and handed Little
Groundhog the gooey seeds, saying,
"We'll dry these in the sun. Then
we can plant them in the spring!"

pumpkin
seeds

cantaloupe
seeds

bell pepper
seeds

potato flowers

potato plant

leek

radish

beet

A chill breeze blew in. "It's time to dig up potatoes," Squirrel said. Little Groundhog watched Squirrel and thought, "That looks like fun!" and so he took a rake and poked around for potatoes, too. When they were finished, Squirrel added composted leaves to her garden as fertilizer for the coming year.

yam

white potato
for boiling

garlic

white potato
for baking

radish

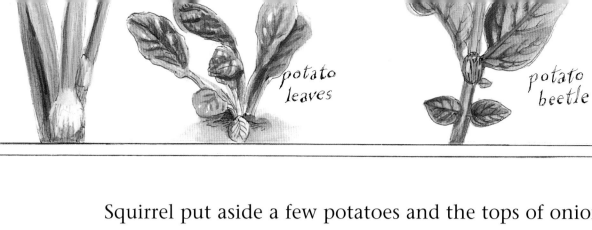

potato
leaves

potato
beetle

turnip

Squirrel put aside a few potatoes and the tops of onions
in a burlap sack. She put the seeds they had collected
in tins to keep them dry
and put the tins
into her sack.

carrot

white
onion

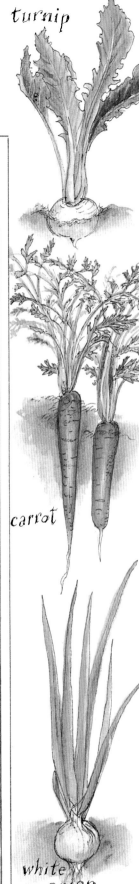

red
potato

yellow
onion

sweet potato

onions

radish

November's snow flurries told Squirrel that winter was on its way.

"Sweet dreams, Little Groundhog," Squirrel said as she curled up in her tree hole.

"See you in the spring," Little Groundhog said, snuggling into his deep earthen burrow. As winter snows blew, Little Groundhog and Squirrel slept.

In February, Little Groundhog awoke and drowsily ambled up to the burrow entrance. The wind made him shiver. He saw his shadow and hurried back inside.

"Oh my," he said. "This will be a long winter."

Weeks later, he awoke with a start. "It's spring!" he shouted, and up he scuttled to the burrow entrance. There he met Squirrel carrying the burlap sack they had filled with potatoes and the tins of seeds.

"Rise and shine!" Squirrel said. "It's planting time! Look! The potatoes are sprouting!"

"First, we'll cut them into little pieces with two sprouts each. Then, we'll plant them with their sprouts pointing up and cover them with soil. Each sprout will grow into a new potato plant. Next fall, we'll dig new potatoes out of the ground. Now let's find a sunny place for your garden!"

When they found a good spot, Squirrel told Little Groundhog,
"First, we need to dig in the soil to loosen it up."
Next, they planted the cut-up potatoes.
Then, they dug rows and sprinkled
in carrot, beet, parsnip,
and radish seeds.

"All these vegetables will grow under the ground,"
Squirrel told him, "so we call them root crops."
   They covered the seeds with dirt and gently
watered them. At the end of each row,
Squirrel stuck markers to help them
remember what they had planted.

bell pepper seeds   pole bean seeds

mustard greens

mung beans

swiss chard

cantaloupe

peas

corn

Squirrel told Little Groundhog, "Plants need lots of sun. We'll plant taller vegetables in the back so they won't cast a shadow over the shorter ones."

So behind the row of root crops, they planted seeds of tomatoes, peppers, and leafy greens.

cilantro   radish   lettuce   lettuce   lettuce   cut-up potato pieces

"Some vegetables grow on vines," said Squirrel. She pounded sticks into the ground for the pea and bean plants to climb.

"Some plants grow very big," said Squirrel. They planted the seeds of pumpkins, zucchini, yellow squash, sunflowers, corn, and artichokes far apart to give them lots of room to grow.

carrot seeds

tomato seeds

onion sets

sweet pepper seeds

eggplant seeds

pole snap bean

cucumber seeds

beet seeds

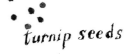
turnip seeds

The next day, Squirrel said, "Let's visit my garden. I want to show you the plants that come up year after year all by themselves. They're called perennials." Sure enough, shoots of raspberries and asparagus were already poking up through the ground.

Squirrel dug up a frilly young asparagus plant for Little Groundhog's garden. She told him, "You'll need to wait three years before this asparagus has nice, thick stems to eat."

Little Groundhog said, "Thank you! I'm off to plant my per-ren-ne-als."

lettuce

bean

cantaloupe

corn

eggplant

cucumber

tomato

Every day, Little Groundhog watched and
waited and watered his garden. Then one day,
tiny seedlings emerged. "What a wonder!" he exclaimed.
But as they grew, he worried. "Are these seedlings too
crowded together? What should I do?" he asked Squirrel.
"Pull some up and plant them somewhere else," she said.

pea

Little Groundhog pulled up a few seedlings and looked at them. The peas, the beans, and all the seeds had split open. From each, a root grew down and a shoot grew up. Little Groundhog transplanted some seedlings where they had more room to grow.

sunflower

syrphid
flower fly

strangalia

blueberry
bee
osmia ribifloris

parasitic
wasp

alfalfa
leaf-cutter bee

metallic
agapostemon
sweat bee

squash
bee

longhorn
beetle

wren

Wren and Praying Mantis said to Little Groundhog,
"If you promise not to harm us with bug spray,
we birds and insects will help you with
your garden. We will eat the harmful
insects that hurt your plants."
Little Groundhog promised.

lightning bug
or
firefly

firefly
larvae

ladybug, ladybird
or ladybeetle

cerotina

male halictid bee

green metallic
bee

earthworm

bumble bee
bombus

female halictid
bee

green
metallic
bee

augochlora
sweat bee

ground beetle

tiger beetle

braconid parasite

thread-waisted wasp

green lacewing

Eastern bluebird

As the weeks passed, plants grew and blossomed. Bees, flies, and butterflies came to eat the sweet nectar and carried pollen from flower to flower. They told Little Groundhog, "The wind, the rain, and we insects pollinate your flowers so they can become fruits and vegetables."

ladybug larvae

ladybug, ladybird or lady beetle

blue orchard bee

megachile leaf-cutting bee

robin

carpenter bee xylocopidae

apis mellifera honeybee

andrena

ladybug, ladybird or lady beetle

Little Groundhog noticed that after a flower
was pollinated by an insect or by the wind, its
petals dried up and fell off. Underneath was the
smallest beginning of a tiny vegetable. . . .

yellow
squash

snow
peas

tomato

pepper

"A tiny tomato! A tiny cucumber! A pepper! An eggplant! A pea pod! A zucchini! So this is how a garden grows!" Little Groundhog cried jubilantly.

eggplant

zucchini

Tomatoes turned red. Heads of cabbage grew. A sunflower seemed to explode from the top of a tall stalk. Snap peas, string beans, peppers, lettuce, and chard grew larger under the warm sun. Little Groundhog rejoiced! He ate his very own vegetables, plain and fresh, from his very own garden all summer long.

When fall came again, Squirrel wanted to share one more secret
with Little Groundhog—cooking. And so they stewed tomatoes, boiled
corn, broiled potatoes, stir-fried veggies, and even stuffed and
baked a zucchini, saving the seeds to plant the next year.
There was so much more than they could eat themselves.
"What do we do?" asked Little Groundhog.
"We share," said Squirrel.

"What a great idea!" cried Little Groundhog.

As they sat around the table, their friends exclaimed, "Thank you for inviting us to this amazing feast!"

Little Groundhog replied, "Thank you all for forgiving me for eating from your gardens last year. And thank you, Squirrel, for teaching me to grow my own! It's beautiful! Scrumptious! Irresistible! Let's eat!"

"What a fortunate creature I am," he thought. "Delicious, nutritious, homegrown food and wonderful friends to share it with."

Little Groundhog grew into a big groundhog and became known far and wide for his annual Thanksgiving dinner. And that is how Groundhog's garden grew!

AUTHOR'S NOTE

Few things in your life will be as important to your health as the food you eat. Good fresh food will nourish you and help protect you from disease. The fresher the food you eat, the healthier you will be.

I have been growing fresh food in my own garden my entire life, and gardening is fascinating. A tiny seed germinates, and a seedling pokes its little head above the earth. Within a month or two, that small plant is a large plant bearing wonderful, delicious vegetables that taste very different from the ones you buy in stores. When you pick a ripe, red, homegrown tomato, it is warm, juicy, and delicious—not hard, pink, and tasteless like some supermarket tomatoes.

I learned from my father and mother what Little Groundhog learns from Squirrel in this story: how to plant seeds and how to care for plants by watering, weeding, and transplanting—and that in order to grow, plants need sunlight, water, and good earth.

As a child, I learned how to enrich the soil with compost—and today I do the same. I watch as leaves, vegetables, and leftover food in the compost pile decompose—rot—seemingly disappear. But they don't really disappear; they just turn into something else—new soil. Watching organic matter rot (biodegrade) in the compost pile and become new earth seems like magic. But it's not magic—it's science; it's LIFE. Insects and other living things, some so small that you can't see them, eat the things you put in the compost pile and turn them into dirt.

I put composted earth in my vegetable garden because compost is rich and nutritious food for plants. Just as the better the food you eat, the healthier you are, the better the "food" the plants have to "eat," the healthier they are—the bigger and stronger they grow, and the better they are able to resist disease and pests.

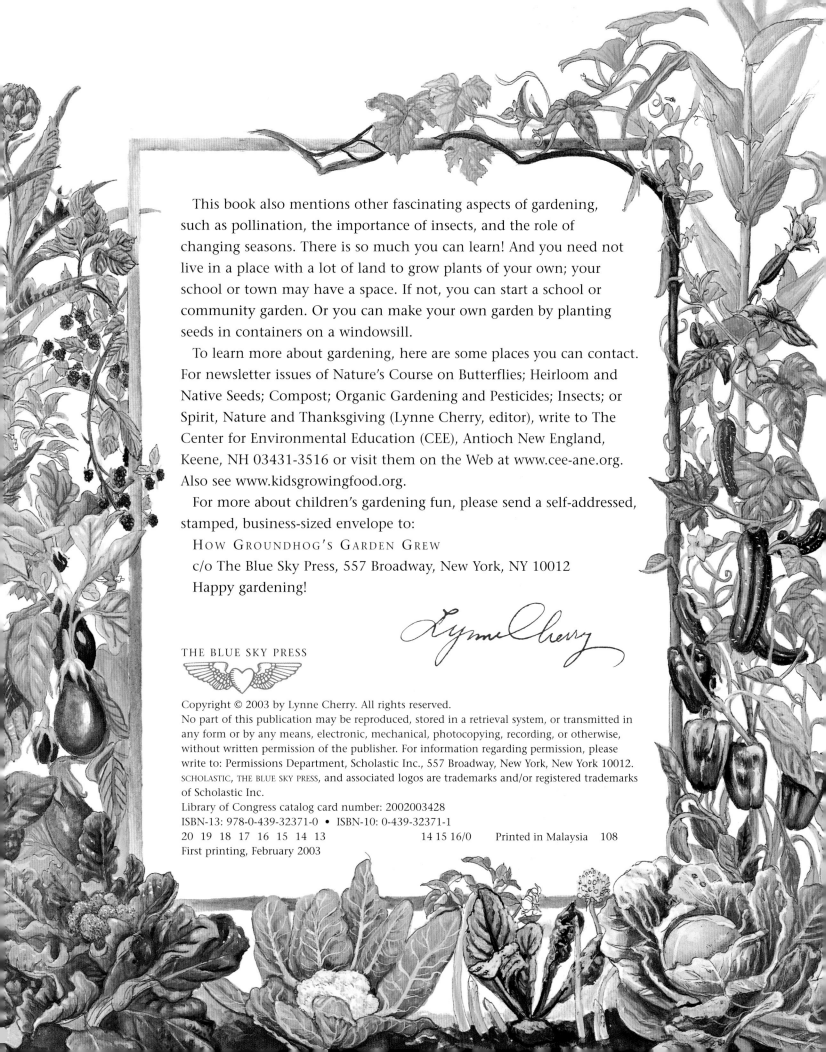

This book also mentions other fascinating aspects of gardening, such as pollination, the importance of insects, and the role of changing seasons. There is so much you can learn! And you need not live in a place with a lot of land to grow plants of your own; your school or town may have a space. If not, you can start a school or community garden. Or you can make your own garden by planting seeds in containers on a windowsill.

To learn more about gardening, here are some places you can contact. For newsletter issues of Nature's Course on Butterflies; Heirloom and Native Seeds; Compost; Organic Gardening and Pesticides; Insects; or Spirit, Nature and Thanksgiving (Lynne Cherry, editor), write to The Center for Environmental Education (CEE), Antioch New England, Keene, NH 03431-3516 or visit them on the Web at www.cee-ane.org. Also see www.kidsgrowingfood.org.

For more about children's gardening fun, please send a self-addressed, stamped, business-sized envelope to:

HOW GROUNDHOG'S GARDEN GREW
c/o The Blue Sky Press, 557 Broadway, New York, NY 10012
Happy gardening!

Lynne Cherry

THE BLUE SKY PRESS

Library of Congress catalog card number: 2002003428

ISBN-13: 978-0-439-32371-0 • ISBN-10: 0-439-32371-1

20 19 18 17 16 15 14 13   14 15 16/0   Printed in Malaysia   108

First printing, February 2003

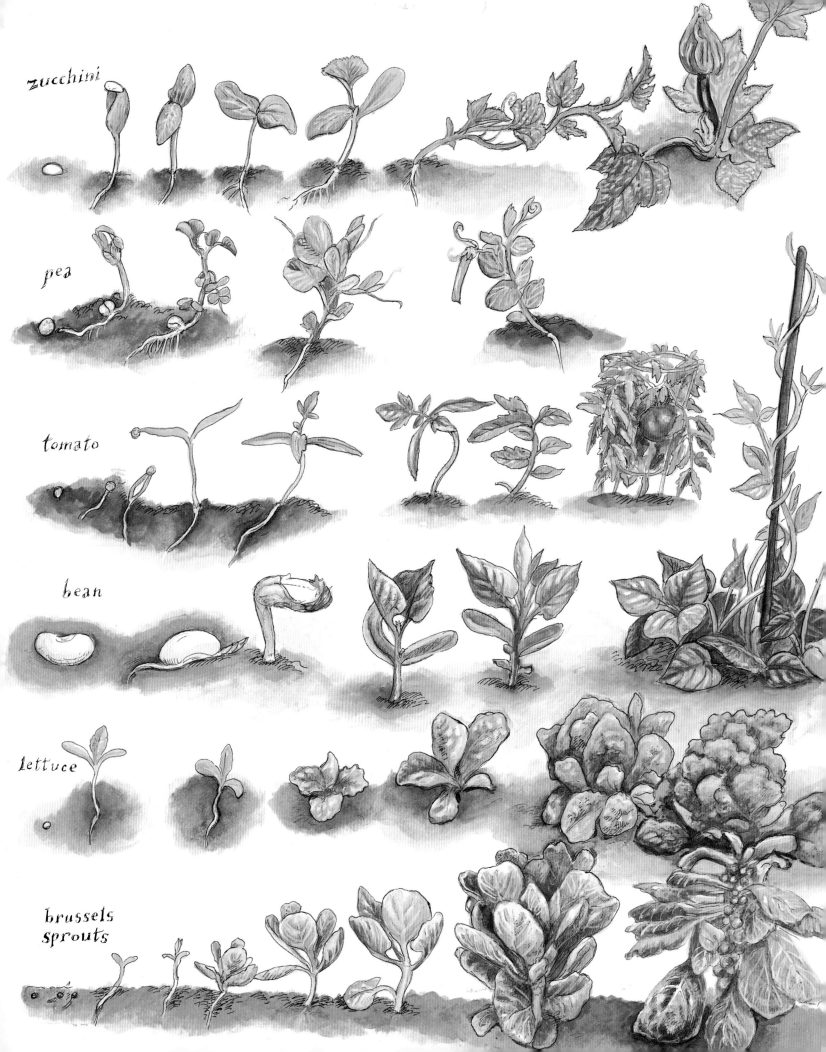

zucchini

pea

tomato

bean

lettuce

brussels
sprouts

zucchini